24 Advent Romance Novels

Your advent calendar of

romantic Christmas stories

Jade Lavoué

Translated into English by Mary Harper.
ISBN : 9798300791865

Contents

Foreword

🎄 Welcome to your Advent Calendar
Christmas stories! 🎄

Hi there! Ready for a magical adventure this Christmas? Then open your eyes wide and get ready to plunge into a world of romance, laughter and winter surprises.

Every day from December 1 to 24, discover a new story that will transport you to the heart of the Christmas spirit. These stories, specially concocted for you, will take you on a journey, make you dream, and maybe even make you fall in love.

From unexpected encounters to magical evenings, from TikTok challenges to Christmas playlists, each story is a window onto a world filled with magic and love. Whether you're looking for inspiration, relaxation or simply a moment of escape, these stories are made for you.

So sit back with your hot chocolate, curl up in your cozy blanket and let yourself be carried away by the magic of these 24 stories. Who knows, maybe you'll find the spark that will light up your Christmas!

🎁 Happy reading and a wonderful Christmas! 🎁

Swipe Right for Christmas

Snow fell softly over the rooftops of Paris, enveloping the city in a peaceful blanket of white. Inside a small, warm apartment, Emma, a 22-year-old art student, was lying on her bed, wrapped in a cozy plaid, her phone in hand. She was scrolling through profiles on a popular dating app, without much conviction. It was Christmas Eve, and instead of attending a noisy party or snuggling with someone under the mistletoe, she was there, alone, with only the twinkling lights of her decorated tree for company.

As she absent-mindedly scanned her phone screen, a profile caught her eye. Max, a 24-year-old photography and travel enthusiast, had a charming smile on his photo. Intrigued, she read his bio, which mentioned his love of science fiction novels and his habit of going for morning runs, even in winter. Something about him seemed strangely familiar, as if they'd crossed paths somewhere before. Without giving it much thought, she slid her finger to the right. "Match" appeared on the screen.

A few seconds later, a notification appeared: "Max has sent a message." Emma opened the conversation, a shy smile forming on her lips.

"Hi Emma, I love your style in your photos. You seem to

have an interesting story. Tell me something unique about yourself?" wrote Max.

Emma hesitated for a moment. She wasn't used to revealing herself so quickly, especially to a stranger. But something in the sincere simplicity of his message encouraged her to respond.

"Hi Max, thanks! Unique, huh? Well, I collect vintage editions of storybooks. And you, what's your least guarded secret?" she replied, her curiosity piqued.

Conversation flowed naturally, oscillating between their passions, their dreams, and even their favorite Christmas dishes. They discovered that they shared not only common hobbies but also a similar outlook on life. Emma felt surprisingly at ease, as if she were talking to an old friend.

As the conversation between Emma and Max intensified, the hours passed unnoticed. They were now sharing anecdotes about their childhoods, their most embarrassing moments, and even their future aspirations. Emma discovered that Max was passionate about the environment and worked for a start-up focused on sustainable development. Max, for his part, was fascinated by Emma's creativity and originality, and aspired to open her own art gallery one day.

At one point, Max proposed, a little shyly: "Listen, I know this is a bit sudden, but I'm organizing a little virtual gift exchange with some online friends tonight. Would you like to join us? We could get to know each other in a slightly more real context."

Emma hesitated. It was unexpected and a little outside her comfort zone. But something inside her told her to take the risk. "Okay, why not?" she replied with a mixture of excitement and nervousness.

That evening, Emma connected via her computer to the videoconference session organized by Max. She was greeted by a group of smiling faces, all warm and welcoming. Max was there, his smile even brighter live. The evening was filled with laughter, sharing of Christmas traditions, and virtual gift exchanges, where everyone presented a meaningful object and told its story.

Emma felt surprisingly at ease, touched by the group's warm welcome and Max's sincere attention. They exchanged glances and smiles throughout the evening, strengthening the bond that had formed between them.

At the end of the evening, Max sent Emma a private message: "I really loved having you here tonight. You're even more incredible in person. Do you think we could meet in person? Maybe a walk in the park tomorrow, if you're free?"

Emma's heart was racing. She knew this was beyond the boundaries of her usual routine, especially with someone she'd just met online. But she felt there was something special between them, a connection worth exploring.

"Yes, I'd love that," she replied, a smile forming on her lips.

The next day, wrapped up in her winter coat, Emma waited for Max in the park. Snow covered everything, making the landscape a serene beauty. When Max arrived, their eyes met and a shiver of excitement ran through Emma. They walked together, talking about everything, laughing and sharing moments of comfortable silence.

The magic of Christmas seemed to float through the air, and as they stopped to admire a large, illuminated fir tree, Max gently took Emma's hand. She looked up at him, her eyes sparkling with happiness.

"It may be a bit of a cliché," Max says with a smile, "but I really believe that this meeting was an unexpected Christmas present."

Emma nodded, sharing his sentiment. "Best Christmas present I could have hoped for," she replied.

The park was quiet, the tree lights twinkling in their eyes, and in that perfect moment, Emma knew she'd made the right choice by swiping right that evening.

.

Christmas playlist

Lucas, 23, a technology consultant with a passion for music, was sitting in his studio in Lyon, browsing the latest music on his computer. It was just a few days before Christmas, and the festive atmosphere was inspiring him. He decided to create a special Christmas playlist, mixing classics with lesser-known tunes and a few surprises. Once satisfied with his selection, he shared the playlist on his social networks, hoping to bring a little joy to his friends and followers.

Among them was Chloé, a 21-year-old graphic design student, who came across Lucas' playlist by chance. Intrigued, she launched it and was immediately captivated by the choice of tracks. She decided to leave a comment under Lucas' post: "Your playlist is incredible! It really brightened up my evening. Thank you!"

Lucas, surprised and delighted to receive such a comment, visited Chloé's profile and was impressed by her design work. He replied, "I'm glad you like it! You've got a hell of a talent for design, I love your style."

This first exchange was the start of a series of messages between Lucas and Chloé. They discovered that they shared a common love of music, art and urban culture. Lucas was fascinated by Chloé's creativity and artistic vision, while Chloé appreciated Lucas's musical sensibility and intellectual curiosity.

One evening, Lucas asked Chloé to collaborate on a new playlist for New Year's Eve. Chloé enthusiastically accepted. They spent hours video-conferencing, sharing tracks, discussing their musical influences, and laughing about their sometimes strange tastes.

After several weeks of online exchanges, Lucas suggested they meet to attend a Christmas concert at a local café. Chloe, though a little nervous, accepted the invitation. She felt there was something special about their connection.

On the day of the concert, Chloé arrived at the café, her heart pounding at the prospect of meeting Lucas in person. When they saw each other, it was as if they'd known each other for a long time. The concert was a perfect blend of jazz, soul and Christmas classics, creating a magical atmosphere.

At the café, Lucas and Chloé found themselves a table close to the stage. The music filled the space, enveloping the place in an atmosphere both intimate and joyous. Between songs, they talked about anything and everything, their conversations flowing as naturally as the music around them. Chloé felt surprisingly at ease with Lucas, finding in him an attentive ear and a kindred spirit.

At one point, Lucas grasped Chloé's hand. "You know," he said softly, "I never thought a simple playlist would lead to such a perfect moment." Chloe smiled at him, squeezing his hand in return. "Music really does have the power to bring people together," she replied.

After the concert, they decided to take a stroll through the city's illuminated streets. Christmas decorations twinkled everywhere, creating a magical atmosphere. They stopped in front of a large Christmas tree in the center of the square, admiring the lights and ornaments.

"It's amazing, isn't it?" said Lucas, looking at the tree. "Just like tonight."

Chloe nodded, feeling moved. "I'm really glad you shared your playlist," she said.

In the next instant, Lucas leaned over to Chloé and kissed her gently under the sparkling lights of the fir tree. It was a gentle kiss, hesitant at first, but quickly becoming more assured. Chloé responded to his kiss, her heart soaring.

After their magical moment under the tree, Lucas and Chloé walked hand in hand, sharing dreams and laughter. They knew something special had begun between them that night.

As the evening drew to a close, Lucas looked Chloe in the eye. "I think we've just started our own life playlist," he said with a smile.

Chloe laughed, a gleam of hope and joy in her eyes. "I can't wait to hear the rest of the pieces," she replied.

Christmas night came to an end, but for Lucas and Chloé, it was the beginning of a beautiful symphony together, a symphony of shared moments, music and love.

.

Winter Hashtags

Aurélie, 20, a communications student in Marseille, loved capturing life's unique moments through her lens. With the arrival of winter, she embarked on a personal project: documenting the joys of winter on her Instagram account. She posted daily photos of snowy landscapes, warm drinks, and wintry urban scenes, accompanied by creative hashtags like #HiverEnVille and #MagieDecembre.

Thomas, a 22-year-old graphic designer living in the same city, came across Aurélie's account while searching for the hashtag #HiverEnVille. He was immediately captivated by the beauty and authenticity of her photos. He began following her account and left a comment under one of her photos: "Your photos capture the spirit of winter perfectly. I love it!"

Aurélie, delighted to receive such a comment, visited Thomas' profile and was impressed by his designs and illustrations. She replied: "Thank you so much! I appreciate your work too. You have an incredible eye for design."

This initial exchange on Instagram quickly turned into a series of comments and direct messages. They discussed their respective passions for photography and design, shared tips and ideas, and even talked about their favorite places in town to capture the essence of winter.

One day, Thomas suggested: "We both seem to enjoy exploring the city. How would you like to go on a photo trip together? I'm sure we could capture some incredible moments."

Aurelie, though a little hesitant at the idea of meeting someone she'd known online, was intrigued. "It could be fun. We could start with the Christmas market?" she replied.

On the appointed day, Aurélie and Thomas met at the Christmas market, a place vibrant with lights, colors and festive sounds. Aurélie, her camera slung over her shoulder, spotted Thomas waiting for her near the entrance, a bright red scarf around his neck. They exchanged a shy but warm smile.

"At last, we meet in real life!" says Thomas, extending his hand. "Ready for our photographic adventure?"

"Absolutely!" replied Aurélie, a shiver of excitement in her voice.

They strolled through the market, sharing laughs and observations, stopping to capture picturesque scenes.

Thomas showed Aurelie how to play with lights to create magical effects, while Aurelie shared her tips for capturing the mood of a moment.

After the market, they decided to stroll along the old port, where the boats were decorated with strings of lights. The reflection of the lights in the water created a magical spectacle.

"It's amazing here," Aurelie murmured, snapping a photo.

"Yes, and even better in good company," Thomas replied, giving him a meaningful look.

Their conversation became more personal, talking about their dreams, their fears, even their failures. They felt surprisingly at ease with each other, as if they'd known each other all their lives.

The evening was drawing to a close, and they were now sitting on a bench, facing the sea, under a starry sky. Aurélie turned to Thomas.

"I didn't expect this outing to be so... special. Thank you for offering," she said, a gentle smile on her lips.

Thomas turned to her. "I think our hashtags have led us to

something real and beautiful," he said.

He took her hand gently, and Aurelie didn't flinch. And so they remained, hand in hand, gazing up at the night sky, aware that something new and exciting was beginning between them.

Streaming Love

Julien and Léa, two long-time friends and roommates in Strasbourg, had always shared a passion for movies, especially during the festive season. One winter evening, when the city was covered in a blanket of snow, they decided to organize a Christmas movie streaming marathon, huddling in the living room with blankets, hot chocolate, and a collection of their favorite festive films.

As they laughed and commented on the scenes, Julien couldn't help noticing how the candlelight made Léa's eyes sparkle. There was something different tonight, something he'd never really noticed before.

As the films progressed, Julien and Léa unconsciously grew closer, their shoulders touching, their laughter mingling. Léa, normally so talkative, was surprisingly silent, lost in thought. She glanced at Julien from time to time, wondering whether the beating of her heart was due to the festive atmosphere or to something deeper.

At one point, their hands brushed against each other as they reached for the remote, and a shiver ran through them both. They exchanged glances, a mixture of surprise and unidentified emotion.

The last film of the evening came to an end, and the room was plunged into a soft darkness, lit only by the Christmas lights. Julien took a deep breath.

"Lea, I have to tell you something," he began, his voice slightly shaky. "I think I feel something more for you than friendship. I don't know since when, but tonight it became obvious to me."

Léa turned to him, her heart beating wildly. "Julien, I have feelings for you too. I wasn't sure how to approach it, but I'm glad you did."

After their revelations, Julien and Léa sat in silence for a while, each absorbing the implications of what they had just shared. The initial tension slowly transformed into a feeling of relief and excitement.

"I don't want this to change everything between us," Julien said softly. "I value our friendship very much."

Léa smiles at him. "So do I, Julien. But I think we could try to see where this goes, without rushing things."

They decided to watch another film, but this time their

emotions were running high. Every laugh, every glance they exchanged seemed to carry a new meaning.

The film over, they turned off the television, the room plunged into a soft darkness, lit only by the flickering light of candles. Julien turned to Léa.

"Do you know what I love most about you, Lea?" he asked. "Your ability to see beauty in little things, in ordinary moments."

Léa felt herself blush. "And you, Julien, you've always been there for me, even in my worst moments. You make me laugh when I don't even want to smile."

They slowly drew closer, their eyes boring into each other. And in a natural movement, Julien placed his lips on Léa's. It was a gentle kiss, hesitant at first. It was a gentle kiss, hesitant at first, but which quickly developed into something deeper, marking the beginning of a new era in their relationship.

After that, they talked for hours, sharing their hopes, fears and dreams for the future. They realized that they had always been more than just friends, but that it had taken time for their feelings to surface.

As the first light of dawn began to illuminate the living room, Julien took Léa's hand. "Whatever the future holds, I'm happy to share it with you," he murmured.

Lea nodded, snuggling up to him. "Me too, Julien. Together, we can face anything."

They fell asleep on the sofa, snuggled together, smiles on their lips, ready to explore this new chapter in their lives, together.

Christmas match

Camille, a 25-year-old freelance graphic designer living in Bordeaux, was always on the lookout for new ways to celebrate the festive season. When she came across an online gift-matching game called "Christmas Match", she was immediately intrigued. The concept was simple: participants were randomly matched and asked to send each other anonymous gifts based on shared profiles and interests.

She signed up, filling out her profile with her tastes in books, music, and art. Soon after, she received a notification: "You've been matched with Alex, from Toulouse."

Camille began exchanging messages with Alex via the platform. They chatted about their passions, exchanged gift ideas, and shared anecdotes about Christmases past. Alex had a sparkling sense of humor and a charming way of looking at life.

The more they talked, the more Camille felt intrigued by this mysterious Alex. There was something about the way he wrote that touched her deeply.

The day of the gift exchange arrived. Camille received a carefully wrapped package. Inside was an art book she'd mentioned she wanted, accompanied by a handwritten note:

"I hope this book inspires you as much as our conversations have inspired me. Merry Christmas, Alex."

Camille was touched by the thought and effort put into the gift. She knew she wanted to know more about Alex, beyond their anonymous exchange.

Camille, driven by a mixture of curiosity and excitement, decided to respond to Alex's note. She sent him a message on the game's platform: "Your gift was perfect, Alex. Thank you for making my Christmas special. I'd really like to know who's behind these messages."

Alex replied quickly, his answer tinged with obvious joy. "I was thinking the same thing. What do you say we meet? I'll be in Bordeaux next week for work."

Camille's heart was pounding. The prospect of meeting Alex in person was both exciting and intimidating.

They met in a cosy café in Bordeaux. Camille arrived a little early, her heart pounding in her chest. When Alex entered, she immediately recognized him from his profile photo. He was taller than she'd imagined, with a warm smile and sparkling eyes.

"Camille?" he asked as he approached.

"Alex!" she replied, rising to greet him.

Their conversation was easy and natural, as if they'd known each other for years. They talked about everything, from their careers to their hobbies, and of course, their experience in the "Christmas Match" game.

As their meeting progressed, it became clear that there was a real connection between them. Camille felt strangely at ease with Alex, and he seemed to feel the same.

"I'm really glad this game brought us together," Alex says, taking a sip of his coffee.

"Me too," Camille replied, a smile lighting up her face. "It's amazing how a simple gift match can lead to something so real."

Their meeting ended with a promise to meet again soon. As they parted, Camille felt a mixture of excitement and anticipation for the future.

On the way home, she couldn't stop thinking about Alex, their conversation, and the possibility of a new story beginning to unfold. She knew one thing for sure: this Christmas would be unforgettable, thanks to a simple "match" that had led to a surprising connection and maybe even love.

Insta memories

Eva, a young teacher living in Nice, was fond of indulging in nostalgia during the festive season. One winter evening, while flipping through old Christmas photos, she had the idea of sharing some of these memories on Instagram. She posted a series of photos of herself and her school friends, reliving the joyous moments of her teenage years.

Among these friends was Hugo, with whom she had lost touch over the years. Hugo, now an engineer in Lyon, stumbled across Eva's photos while browsing his news feed. The memories of their friendship came back to him with a wave of nostalgia.

He left a comment under one of the photos: "Wow, it's been forever! Remember that Christmas party when we all dressed up?"

Eva, surprised and delighted to see an old friend, replied: "Of course I remember! It was a memorable night. How are you, Hugo?"

This first comment triggered a series of messages between Eva and Hugo. They updated each other on their lives, sharing their successes, challenges and dreams. Eva discovered that Hugo had followed an impressive professional path, while Hugo was fascinated by Eva's passion for teaching.

They began to exchange messages more frequently, recalling childhood memories and anecdotes from their current lives. There was an ease and familiarity in their exchanges, as if time and distance had never existed.

After several weeks of online conversations, Hugo suggested that they meet in person during his next visit to Nice. "It would be great to see each other again and catch up," he wrote.

Eva accepted enthusiastically, her heart pounding at the thought of seeing Hugo again. She wondered if they'd always recognize each other, if their childhood friendship would stand the test of time.

The day of their meeting arrived. Eva was waiting for Hugo at their old favorite café, a place full of memories of their adolescence. When she saw him approach, she was struck by the change in him. He had matured, but his smile and sparkling eyes were still the same.

"Hugo!" she exclaimed, rising to greet him.

"Eva! You haven't changed a bit!" said Hugo, greeting her with a warm embrace.

They ordered coffees and started talking, laughing and swapping stories as if they'd never parted. Their conversation flowed naturally, and they found themselves sharing dreams and aspirations they'd never expressed to anyone else.

As the afternoon wore on, Eva and Hugo realized that they shared more than just childhood memories. They discovered that they shared similar values and life goals, and that their old friendship had evolved into a deeper, more meaningful connection.

"I'm really happy that Instagram has brought us together again," says Hugo, taking a sip of his coffee. "I never imagined that sharing memories would bring us here."

"Me neither," Eva replied, a radiant smile on her face. "It's as if we were destined to meet again."

The sun was beginning to set, tinting the sky with shades of orange and pink. Hugo and Eva knew that this meeting marked the beginning of a new chapter in their lives.

"How about we continue exploring the city together?" proposed Hugo. "There's so much I'd like to show you."

Eva nodded enthusiastically. "I'd love that."

They left the café together, promising to see each other again soon. Walking through the streets of Nice, Eva felt incredibly lucky. This sharing of memories on Instagram had rekindled a precious friendship and opened the door to new adventures and maybe even love.

Selfie in the Snow

Clara, a 22-year-old marketing student in Annecy, loved outdoor adventures, especially in winter. One snowy day, while hiking in the mountains, she decided to capture the winter beauty with a selfie. She posted the photo on Instagram with the hashtag #AventureHivernale, showing off her dazzling smile with a landscape of snow and mountains in the background.

Maxime, a nature and photography enthusiast, saw Clara's selfie by chance while scrolling through Instagram. Impressed by the scenery and captivated by her smile, he left a comment: "Great photo! Winter looks good on you."

Clara, intrigued by this comment, visited Maxime's profile. She was immediately drawn to his photos of landscapes and outdoor adventures. She replied: "Thanks! I love winter. Your photos are amazing too, it looks like you love adventure as much as I do."

This initial exchange on Instagram quickly turned into a series of messages. Clara and Maxime shared a common passion for nature and exploration, which quickly brought them closer together.

They discussed their favorite places to hike, exchanged tips on landscape photography, and talked about past adventures. There was an ease to their conversation that felt both natural and exciting.

One day, Maxime made a bold proposal: "We should go hiking together one of these days. I know some incredible places here in the Alps."

Clara was hesitant at first about meeting someone she'd known online, but the idea of a new adventure with someone who shared her interests was too tempting. "It could be fun. I'm up for it!" she replied.

The day of their hike arrived. Clara and Maxime met at the foot of the mountains, a clear blue sky and a carpet of fresh snow greeting them. Clara recognized Maxime immediately from his profile photos. He had a warm smile and eyes that sparkled with enthusiasm.

"Hi Clara, ready for the adventure?" asked Maxime, his voice full of excitement.

"More than ready!" replied Clara, a bright smile on her face.

They began their ascent, talking about anything and everything. Conversation flowed, and they soon found themselves laughing and sharing personal stories.

At the summit, they were greeted by a breathtaking view. The snow-capped peaks glistened in the sunlight, a breathtaking sight. Clara took out her phone to take a selfie of the two of them, immortalizing the moment.

"This place is amazing," Clara says, admiring the view. "And it's even better to share it with someone."

Maxime nodded, his gaze settling on her. "I'm really glad I commented on your photo. Otherwise, I'd never have experienced this moment."

There was a moment of silence, when they looked at each other, an unspoken feeling floating between them. It was a mixture of gratitude, joy and perhaps even something deeper.

As the day drew to a close, they came back down together, sharing laughs and plans for future adventures. They both knew that this day had marked the beginning of something special.

As they parted, Maxime gently took Clara's hand. "I hope there will be many more adventures for us," he said softly.

Clara smiled, her eyes shining with hope and affection. "Me too, Maxime. Me too."

They parted with the feeling of having begun a new chapter in their lives, a chapter full of promise and shared discoveries, initiated by a simple selfie under the snow.

Midnight Tweet

Sophie, a young journalist based in Paris, used to share her thoughts and experiences on Twitter (X). On New Year's Eve, as she prepared to celebrate alone at home, she decided to tweet: "Who else spends New Year's Eve in pajamas with a pizza? #SoiréeSoloDeNoël".

This tweet caught the attention of Damien, a graphic designer also living in Paris. He humorously replied: "I'll take the challenge. Checked pajamas and Christmas socks. Are we competing? #NoëlEnSolo".

Intrigued and amused, Sophie replied: "Challenge accepted! But I warn you, my pajamas have reindeer on them. #ChristmasInPyjamas".

What began as a light-hearted and amusing exchange soon turned into a series of tweets and replies. Sophie and Damien discovered that they had much in common, including a love of humor, pop culture and the city of Paris.

They spent the evening tweeting, sharing jokes, anecdotes about Christmases past, and even photos of their lonely New Year's Eve meals.

As midnight approached, Damien had a bold idea. He

tweeted: "How about leaving the virtual world behind? I'm having a little brunch tomorrow. You're invited. #RencontreRéelle".

Sophie was surprised by the proposal. It was unusual for her to meet someone from Twitter in real life, but something about their conversation had put her at ease. After a brief hesitation, she replied: "Why not? It'll be my Christmas adventure. #ChristmasBrunch".

The next morning, Sophie headed for the café where Damien had suggested we meet. Excitement mixed with a hint of nervousness made her smile. She wondered what Damien would look like in person and how their meeting would go.

When she arrived at the café, she immediately recognized Damien from his Twitter profile photo. He was sitting at a table by the window, looking both relaxed and attentive. "Sophie?" he asked, rising to greet her.

"Damien!" she replied with a smile. "In the flesh."

They ordered brunch, and the conversation flowed as naturally as it had online. They laughed, shared stories and discovered the little nuances that didn't show up in their tweets.

As their brunch continued, Sophie and Damien felt more and more at ease with each other. There was an undeniable chemistry between them, a connection that went far beyond social networking.

"It's rare to find someone you can laugh with so easily," says Damien, a sincere smile on his lips.

"I agree," Sophie replied. "I didn't expect a tweet to lead me here, but I'm glad it did."

Brunch was drawing to a close, but neither Sophie nor Damien seemed to want the meeting to end. They decided to take a stroll through the streets of Paris, enjoying the city's post-Christmas atmosphere.

As they strolled along, they discussed their hopes and dreams and what the future might hold. It seemed that a door had opened to new possibilities, a chance to discover something deeper and more meaningful.

In parting, Damien says: "I'm really glad we decided to

meet. I hope there will be other opportunities."

Sophie nodded, a feeling of contentment washing over her. "Me too, Damien. Me too."

They parted with the feeling of having started something special, an unexpected adventure initiated by a simple midnight tweet.

.

Christmas Vlog

Léon, a travel vlogger based in Marseille, was known for his captivating videos and tales of adventure around the world. For Christmas, he decided to create something different and proposed a collaboration with another vlogger for a special "Christmas Vlog".

Alice, a lifestyle vlogger from Lyon with a penchant for interior decoration and Christmas DIYs, accepted Léon's invitation. She was enthusiastic about the idea of combining their worlds to create something unique.

They began planning their collaboration via video calls, sharing ideas on content, style and how to capture the Christmas spirit.

Their first meeting took place in Lyon, where they decided to film part of the vlog. Right from the start, they realized that they shared a natural chemistry, both in front of the camera and in their off-camera conversations.

As they explored Christmas markets and illuminated streets, their exchanges were spontaneous and full of energy, making their content authentic and engaging.

As they worked on the vlog, Léon and Alice discovered

that they had a lot in common. They shared a passion for creativity, a love of life's little joys and a similar sense of humor.

They spent hours discussing their vision of vlogging, their personal aspirations and what Christmas meant to them. There was an ease and depth to their exchanges that surprised them both.

As Léon and Alice continued to film across Lyon, their complicity was reflected in every shot, every dialogue. Their Christmas vlog was taking shape, mixing scenes of decorating, festive cooking and strolls through Christmas markets. Their enthusiasm and joy were contagious, promising success with their respective subscribers.

One evening, after a day's shooting, they met for a hot chocolate in a cosy café. It was a quiet moment, a contrast to the hustle and bustle of the day.

"I didn't expect this collaboration to be so... special," Alice admitted, a shy smile on her lips.

Léon nodded, "Me neither. Working with you is easy, natural. It's like we've known each other forever."

In the warm, illuminated atmosphere of the café, they drew closer, sharing personal stories and laughter. There was a chill in the air, a gentle, pleasant tension.

"I have to confess something," Leon began, hesitantly. "I feel something for you, something more than friendship or professional collaboration."

Alice looked at him, her eyes shining with a similar emotion. "I feel the same way, Leon. I was just too nervous to admit it."

That evening marked a turning point in their relationship. What had started as a simple vlog collaboration had turned into something much deeper.

They decided to finish the vlog together, subtly integrating their new relationship into the narrative. Their final video was a perfect blend of joy, creativity and budding love.

The "Christmas Vlog" was a huge success, but for Léon and Alice, the real gift was the discovery of their love, an unexpected alchemy born of a festive collaboration.

Virtual Coffee

Emma, a literature student in Rennes, France, discovered a virtual coffee application designed to connect people with similar interests for online conversations over a virtual cup of coffee. Intrigued, she created a profile, sharing her interests in poetry, art cinema and travel.

Soon after, she was introduced to Julien, a Parisian graphic designer with a taste for writing and music. They began chatting via the app, exchanging ideas on their favorite subjects and sharing personal stories.

Their online conversations quickly became a key part of their day. Emma found in Julien a sympathetic ear and a compatible mind, while Julien was fascinated by Emma's perspective and passion for literature.

They met regularly on the virtual coffee app, sometimes for hours at a time, losing themselves in deep, animated discussions.

As the days went by, their curiosity about each other grew, as did their desire to meet in person. Julien plucked up the courage to propose: "What if we turned our virtual coffee into a real meeting? I'll be in Rennes for the vacations."

Emma's heart leapt at the proposal. She was both nervous and excited at the idea of turning their digital connection into a physical reality. "I'd love that," she replied.

On the day they met, Emma was waiting for Julien in a cosy café in the center of Rennes, her heart pounding with anticipation. When she saw him through the window, she immediately recognized him from their many virtual coffee sessions. Julien was exactly as she had imagined him, with a friendly smile and a reassuring presence.

"Emma?" asked Julien as he entered, his smile widening as he saw her.

"Julien!" she replied, rising to greet him.

They ordered coffee and started talking, quickly finding the same comfort and ease they had online. The conversation flowed naturally, punctuated by laughter and sharing.

As they talked, Emma and Julien realized that their virtual chemistry translated perfectly into the real world. They had so much in common, and their connection seemed even stronger face-to-face.

"I feel like I've known you forever," Julien said, his eyes shining with genuine emotion.

"I feel the same way," Emma replied, her heart light.

They spent the afternoon together, strolling through the streets of Rennes, talking about everything and nothing, like old friends.

Time passed quickly, and soon it was time to part. Julien took Emma's hand. "I don't want it to end here. Can we meet again?" he asked.

Emma nodded, a radiant smile on her face. "I'd love that."

They parted with the promise of seeing each other again, each with the feeling that this meeting was the start of something special. What had begun as a simple virtual coffee had turned into a real and promising connection, a budding romance in this vacation season.

..

Carpooling Adventures

Thomas, a young professional working in Lyon, decided on a whim to join his family for the Christmas holidays in the south of France. Not wanting to travel alone, he posted an advert on a car-sharing app, offering places in his car to Nice.

Marine, an art student, was looking for a way to get home to Nice after spending the semester in Lyon. When she saw Thomas' advert, she didn't hesitate and booked a place. She liked the idea of sharing a ride with someone and, who knows, making a new friend.

Thomas greeted Marine with a friendly smile as she got into his car. From the start of the journey, they discovered that they shared many interests, including a passion for music and travel.

Their conversation was light and amusing, filled with anecdotes and laughter. Marine was impressed by Thomas's ease of communication and already felt at ease in his company.

As they went along, the landscape changed, providing a magnificent backdrop for their journey. They stopped to take photos, share snacks and even listen to music together.

This carpooling trip became an adventure in itself, a series of small shared moments that wove the threads of a budding friendship.

As the journey continued, Thomas and Marine became increasingly comfortable with each other. They shared stories of their childhoods, future aspirations and life experiences. Each story added a layer of mutual understanding and respect.

During a break in a picturesque little town, they decided to take a stroll and discover the Christmas decorations. The festive atmosphere enveloped them, strengthening their budding bond.

As they stood in front of a large, illuminated Christmas tree, Marine turned to Thomas. "I didn't expect this trip to be so enjoyable. I'm really happy to have shared this adventure with you," she said, a sincere smile lighting up her face.

Thomas looked at her, touched by her words. "Me too, Marine. It's one of the best decisions I've ever made."

In a spontaneous moment, he took her hand. Marine didn't pull away, her eyes shining with shared emotion.

The rest of the journey was spent in a warm and comfortable atmosphere. When they finally arrived in Nice, they both knew that something special had happened on the way.

Saying goodbye, Thomas suggested, "We should get together again, don't you think? Maybe after the holidays?"

Marine nodded enthusiastically. "I'd love that."

They parted with a sense of anticipation and hope. What had begun as a simple carpool ride had turned into the beginning of an unexpected friendship and perhaps even something deeper.

Christmas in Augmented Reality

Alex, a game developer with a passion for augmented reality, decided to create a unique experience for the Christmas market in his home town, Toulouse. He developed an augmented reality treasure hunt application, allowing users to discover virtual clues hidden around the market, leading to a final "treasure".

Élise, an art teacher who loved exploring new technologies, downloaded the application after hearing about this innovative treasure hunt. Intrigued by the concept, she went to the Christmas market to give it a try.

As Élise explored the market, following the application's clues, she noticed Alex, who was supervising the experience and helping users. Their eyes met several times, and a smile grew between them.

Having found the last clue, Élise approached Alex to share her impressions. "It's really a great idea. Augmented reality brings a whole new dimension to the Christmas market experience," she said enthusiastically.

Alex was touched by her interest. "Thank you! I wanted to make the market more interactive. It's great to see that people like it."

They continued to talk, sharing their passion for technology, art and innovation. Alex offered to show Élise more of the app's features, and together they explored the market, sharing laughs and discoveries.

Their connection was palpable. Every clue they found brought them a little closer together, forging a link between the virtual world and their reality.

As they progressed through the game, Alex and Élise discovered surprising common interests. They talked about art, literature and the infinite possibilities offered by technology in these fields. The Christmas market, with its twinkling lights and colorful stalls, provided the perfect backdrop for their lively conversation.

At every stand they visited, the game revealed hidden information and fun facts, making their experience even richer. They were like two children discovering a new world, one where reality and the virtual blended harmoniously.

After completing the treasure hunt, they found themselves in front of the market's large Christmas tree, its glow magnified by the augmented reality application. Alex took out his phone to show Élise how the tree came to life with virtual effects.

"Look," he says, "augmented reality can make things even more magical."

Élise watched in wonder. Then she turned to Alex, her eyes shining with emotion. "You know, it's not just augmented reality that makes tonight magical," she murmured.

Alex looked at her, a shiver running down his spine. He felt something special, a feeling that went beyond admiration for her application.

The market was beginning to close, but they didn't want the evening to end. Alex suggested they go for a drink in a nearby café to prolong their meeting.

Sitting in the café, surrounded by soft candlelight, they talked about their dreams and future plans. It was clear that their meeting was no accident, but the beginning of a deeper story.

As they parted, they exchanged numbers, a knowing smile

on their lips. "I'd really like to see you again," said Alex.

"I want to, too," replied Élise, with a light heart.

Their augmented reality adventure had turned into a real-life connection, promising new discoveries and perhaps even the start of a beautiful love story.

Love podcast

Lucie, host of a popular podcast about love stories, decided to do a special episode for Christmas. She wanted to invite an unknown person to share their experience or dream of love during the holidays. After a call for applications, she was intrigued by the response from Jérôme, an amateur writer with a passion for Christmas tales.

When they met to record the podcast, Lucie was immediately captivated by Jérôme's warm voice and natural charm. He enthusiastically recounted his Christmas stories, mixing humor and tenderness.

During the recording, Lucie and Jérôme discovered that they shared a love for stories that touch the heart. Their exchanges were fluid and full of spontaneous complicity.

Their conversation gradually drifted away from the initial topic to address their personal experiences, passions and aspirations. There was an undeniable chemistry between them, a connection that went beyond the studio microphones.

Once the recording was over, they didn't want to leave each other. Lucie suggested to Jérôme that they continue their conversation over coffee. Jérôme accepted enthusiastically, curious to learn more about the woman behind the podcast's voice.

Sitting in a nearby café, surrounded by the festive atmosphere, they shared their stories, laughing and discovering each other. Their conversation flowed naturally, as if they'd known each other for a long time.

In the café, Lucie and Jérôme continued to discuss their lives, sharing anecdotes and dreams. Lucie was fascinated by Jérôme's way of seeing the world, by his optimism and his ability to find beauty in small things.

Jérôme, for his part, was impressed by Lucie's passion and intelligence. He loved the way she listened, her infectious laugh and the way she saw beyond appearances.

As the evening wore on, they realized that they didn't want the moment to end. There was a budding feeling between them, something deeper than simple friendship.

"I feel really lucky to have been chosen for your podcast," Jerome says, a tender smile on his lips. "I never imagined that it would lead me to meet someone like you."

Lucie blushed slightly. "Me neither," she confessed. "I think it's the best interview I've ever done."

As they parted, they exchanged numbers, promising to meet again. As they parted, a feeling of excitement and anticipation enveloped them. They both knew that something unique and special had just begun.

The Christmas podcast was a success, but for Lucie and Jérôme, the real gift was their meeting and the promise of a budding love story, born of spontaneous sharing and genuine connection.

Livestream meeting

Mélanie, a content creator with a passion for the festive season, decided to launch a livestream on her YouTube channel dedicated to Christmas preparations. She wanted to share decorating ideas, cooking recipes and tips for a perfect Christmas with her community.

Among the many viewers, Éric, a passionate fan of cooking and Christmas traditions, was captivated by Mélanie's livestream. He was impressed by her creativity and energy, and decided to leave a comment: "Great decorating ideas! I love your style."

Melanie saw Eric's comment and replied live, a beaming smile on her lips. "Thank you so much! Glad you liked it. Do you have any Christmas traditions to share?"

This first live livestream exchange triggered a series of discussions between Mélanie and Éric. They shared ideas, Christmas memories and even jokes, creating a fun and engaging dynamic for the other viewers.

Éric was increasingly attracted to Mélanie, not only by her creativity but also by her warm and welcoming personality. Mélanie, for her part, was curious to find out more about this interactive and attentive spectator.

After several exchanges during various livestreams, Mélanie spontaneously proposed that Éric join her for a special Christmas livestream. "It might be fun to cook together live. What do you think?" she suggested.

Éric enthusiastically accepted the invitation, delighted by the opportunity to meet Mélanie in person and share her passion for Christmas cooking.

The day of the special Christmas livestream arrived. Mélanie welcomed Éric into her kitchen, carefully decorated for the occasion. From the very first moment, their complicity was obvious, both on and off the screen. They laughed, shared anecdotes and cooked together, creating a warm and festive atmosphere.

Their chemistry was palpable, and livestream viewers were quick to notice, leaving enthusiastic and encouraging comments. Mélanie and Éric were a dynamic duo, their shared passion for Christmas illuminating the broadcast.

After the livestream, Mélanie and Éric stayed to chat, discovering even more about each other. They realized they had a lot in common, far beyond their passions for Christmas and cooking.

There was a natural attraction between them, a sense of comfort and familiarity that surprised them both. "I never expected a livestream to lead to such a connection," Melanie confessed, a shy smile on her lips.

"Nor me," replied Eric. "But I'm really glad you did."

As they parted, they exchanged numbers, promising to see each other again soon. As they parted, they felt excited and happy, aware that they had just experienced something unique.

The Christmas livestream had been a success, but what they had gained was far more precious: the beginning of a love story, born under the twinkling Christmas lights and before the eyes of their online community.

Love Code Line

Clara and Maxime, two programming enthusiasts, met at a Christmas hackathon organized in their home town, Nantes. The theme was to create innovative applications around the holiday spirit. Clara, an expert in artificial intelligence, and Maxime, a web development specialist, were assigned to the same team by pure chance.

Right from the start, they discovered that they shared a similar approach to programming: creative, rigorous and humorous.

As they worked on their project, an app that personalized Christmas songs according to the user's tastes, Clara and Maxime found themselves naturally in sync. They complemented each other's ideas, helping each other with technical challenges and laughing at each other's mistakes.

Their complicity was obvious to all involved. Between the lines of code and the debugging sessions, a friendship was born, based on mutual respect and a shared passion.

As the hours passed, Clara and Maxime grew closer, sharing personal anecdotes and dreams. They were impressed by each other's talents and personalities.

In the frenzy of the hackathon, an unexpected attraction developed. Clara found in Maxime an intelligence and sensitivity she'd never encountered before. Maxime, for his part, was captivated by Clara's quick wit and ability to solve complex problems.

The hackathon continued throughout the night, with teams working non-stop. In the atmosphere of concentration and coffee, Clara and Maxime found a moment of respite. Sitting side by side, they shared a pizza, exhausted but exhilarated.

"It's crazy, I've never felt so connected to someone during a hackathon," says Maxime, a tired smile on his lips.

Clara nodded. "Me neither. It's like we understand each other without even speaking." There was a gleam in her eyes that spoke volumes about her budding feelings.

As dawn broke, their project took shape, a harmonious blend of their skills and ideas. They were proud of their work, but something deeper bound them together.

In the final hours of the hackathon, as they were putting the finishing touches to their app, Clara made a bold decision. "Maxime, I'd like us to keep seeing each other, outside of code and hackathons. Just you and me."

Maxime looked at her, his heart racing. "I was thinking exactly the same thing. I'd really like that."

The hackathon drew to a close. Their project was well received, but for Clara and Maxime, the real prize was the relationship they had forged. They left the event with a promise to meet again soon, eager to explore the possibilities of this new connection.

Their meeting at the Christmas hackathon was unexpected, but paved the way for a passionate love affair based on mutual understanding and deep admiration.

Winter Photography

Sarah, a freelance photographer based in Strasbourg, was passionate about winter landscapes and festive portraits. To expand her portfolio, she posted an advert on an online platform, seeking volunteers for a Christmas photo shoot in her city, renowned for its fairytale Christmas market.

Marc, a graphic designer and photography enthusiast, came across Sarah's ad. Intrigued by her work and seduced by the idea of a winter photo shoot, he answered the ad, offering to collaborate as model and assistant.

Their first meeting took place in a café near the Christmas market. Sarah was immediately struck by Marc's natural charisma and interest in photography. Marc, for his part, was fascinated by Sarah's artistic vision and the way she captured the magic of winter.

They discussed the details of the shoot, sharing ideas and planning locations. There was an immediate creative chemistry between them, a connection based on their shared passion for visual art.

On the day of the shoot, Strasbourg was covered in a white coat, with Christmas lights adding a magical touch to the city. Sarah and Marc worked together, capturing enchanting winter scenes and portraits where Marc naturally shone.

Throughout the session, their complicity grew. They laughed, shared moments of contemplative silence and appreciated the beauty all around them.

After several hours of shooting in the snowy streets of Strasbourg, Sarah and Marc decided to take a break in a cozy café. Over hot chocolate, they exchanged stories about their lives, dreams and inspirations.

Marc was captivated by Sarah's energy and creativity, while Sarah found in Marc a deep sensitivity and understanding. Their conversation was fluid and natural, as if they'd known each other for years.

As night fell on Strasbourg, illuminated by Christmas lights, Sarah and Marc realized that they didn't want the day to end. There was something special in the air, a budding feeling they were both reluctant to name, but impossible to ignore.

"I'm really glad I answered your ad," Marc said, his gaze locked in Sarah's. "I didn't expect to find such a connection."

Sarah smiled at him, "Me neither. Today was amazing. More than just a photo shoot."

Their day ended with a promise to meet again soon. As they parted, Sarah and Marc knew that something unique had begun between them. Not just an artistic collaboration, but the beginning of a romantic story.

They parted with the promise of future photo sessions and other shared moments. The Christmas photo session had been the spark for a budding romance, a love story in the making, born in the heart of winter and under the twinkling Christmas lights.

Blog exchanges

Emma, who ran a blog on world traditions and cultures, had the idea of writing a series of posts on Christmas traditions around the world. To give her project a more personal dimension, she decided to collaborate with other bloggers.

One of the bloggers who answered her call was Lucas, an avid traveler and cook, who blogged about his culinary adventures around the world. Intrigued by Emma's idea, he offered to share his own Christmas experiences and recipes.

Through their exchange of emails and blog posts, Emma and Lucas discovered that they had a lot in common. They shared a love of tradition, a curiosity about different cultures and a passion for writing.

Their posts were a mix of personal stories, descriptions of Christmas traditions and family recipes. Their readers were captivated by this collaboration, which brought a personal and authentic touch to their respective blogs.

Over the course of their exchanges, a chemistry developed between Emma and Lucas. Their writings revealed a mutual understanding and appreciation, and each post seemed to strengthen their connection.

They began to share more than just information about Christmas traditions. Personal anecdotes, dreams and aspirations intertwined in their correspondence, making their interaction ever deeper and more meaningful.

As Christmas approached, Emma and Lucas felt closer and closer, even though they'd never met in person. Their online exchanges had become the highlight of their days, a mixture of anticipation and excitement.

One evening, as they were discussing Christmas traditions in their respective families, Lucas wrote something that touched Emma deeply: "Through our posts, I feel like I'm traveling with you, discovering new horizons. It's an incredible feeling."

Emma felt moved by his words. She replied, "Me too, Lucas. I wish one day we could share these traditions together, for real."

Driven by a mutual desire to meet, Emma and Lucas decided to organize a real-life get-together. They chose a Christmas market halfway between their two cities, a perfect place to celebrate the traditions they had shared on their blogs.

On the day they met, excitement was running high. When they finally saw each other, it was as if characters from their blogs had come to life. They exchanged a knowing smile and a look of recognition.

The Christmas market was an idyllic setting for their first meeting. They strolled among the stalls, sharing hot chestnuts and stories as if they'd known each other all their lives.

At the end of the day, Lucas took Emma's hand. "Meeting in person is even better than I imagined. I don't want it to end."

Emma smiled, her heart racing. "Me neither. This is just the beginning, isn't it?"

They parted with a promise to continue writing together, and to meet again soon. Their collaboration had ignited sparks, and now a love affair was beginning to take shape, enriched by their shared traditions and cultures.

Christmas in VR

Antoine, a game developer with a passion for virtual reality, created an immersive VR Christmas experience for an online platform. The experience allowed users to wander through a virtual Christmas village, interact with characters and even take part in festive activities.

Julie, a graphic designer and fan of immersive technologies, discovered Antoine's VR Christmas experience and was immediately captivated. She downloaded the application and plunged into the virtual world created by Antoine, amazed by its realism and creativity.

In the virtual village, Julie met the character Antoine, who guided users through the experience. They began chatting in-game, sharing their impressions and ideas about virtual reality.

Their connection was surprisingly strong, even in this virtual space. They met regularly in the virtual Christmas village, exploring together and sharing moments of joy and laughter.

Over time, Antoine and Julie realized that they wanted to meet in real life. Their virtual interactions had created a strong bond, but they were curious to see if this connection would translate into the real world.

Antoine took the initiative of proposing a meeting. "How about meeting for real? I think it would be amazing to share our passion for VR in person," he wrote.

Julie accepted enthusiastically, eager to turn their virtual friendship into a real relationship.

On the day they met, Antoine was waiting for Julie in a café near a square lit up by Christmas decorations. Excitement and a touch of nervousness filled him. When Julie arrived, Antoine was immediately struck by her smile, which was even brighter in person.

"Julie!" exclaimed Antoine. "It's amazing to see you outside the virtual world."

"Antoine!" replied Julie with a beaming smile. "I'm so glad we took the step to meet."

Sitting in the café, surrounded by the festive atmosphere, their conversation flowed naturally. They talked about their passion for virtual reality, but also about their personal interests, dreams and aspirations.

The connection they had felt online was even stronger in person. They discovered that they shared not only a passion for technology, but also similar values and outlooks on life.

As the evening wore on, neither Antoine nor Julie wanted their encounter to end. They decided to stroll through the illuminated city streets, enjoying the magical Christmas atmosphere.

"I'm really glad we met, first in RV and now here," said Antoine, as they admired the Christmas lights.

"Me too," Julie replied. "This seems to be the beginning of something special."

As they parted, they promised to meet again soon. What had begun as a virtual reality experience had led to a real encounter and the promise of a beautiful story to come, uniting two souls sharing the same passion.

Love in Playlist

Léo and Chloé, two DJs with a passion for electronic music, met at a meeting to organize a major Christmas party in their city, Bordeaux. They were asked to work together to create a collaborative playlist that would be the musical heart of the event.

Léo was known for his dynamic, upbeat sets, while Chloé had a reputation as an innovative DJ, mixing a variety of genres in her mixes. Intrigued by the challenge, they agreed to collaborate.

From their very first working session, Léo and Chloé discovered that they had an incredible musical chemistry. Their musical tastes complemented each other perfectly, and their ideas intertwined to create unique mixes.

They spent hours listening to tracks, discussing transitions and experimenting with different genres. Each session was a mixture of hard work and moments of pure pleasure.

Beyond the music, Léo and Chloé began to discover each other. They shared life stories, dreams and aspirations. Chloé was fascinated by Léo's passion for music and his artistic approach. Léo, for his part, admired Chloé's creativity and musical daring.

Their collaboration became something more personal. They felt a connection that went beyond their musical project.

As Christmas approached, Léo and Chloé spent more and more time together, fine-tuning their playlist. One evening, after a long work session, they found themselves talking about their personal lives, exchanging confidences in the quiet of the studio.

Leo took a deep breath and launched himself. "Chloé, I have to admit something to you. Working with you on this project has been one of the best experiences of my life. I feel something more for you."

Chloe looked at him, surprised but obviously touched. "Leo, I feel the same way. I wasn't sure how to approach it, but I'm glad you did."

Their mutual confession opened the door to a new level in their relationship. They began spending time together outside the studio, discovering that they shared much more than their love of music.

On Christmas Eve, their playlist was a resounding success. The crowd danced to the rhythm of their mixes, and between songs Léo and Chloé exchanged knowing glances, their connection obvious to all.

After the party, as the last notes of music faded, Léo and Chloé found themselves alone, a feeling of success and happiness enveloping them.

"This is just the beginning, isn't it?" asked Chloe, taking Leo's hand.

"Absolutely," Leo replied with a smile. "I think we make a perfect duo, both in music and in life."

They vowed to continue creating playlists and memories together. Their musical collaboration had led to an unexpected romance, a love born of shared passion and Christmas melodies.

Christmas TikTok Challenge

Élodie, a young content creator on TikTok, was always on the lookout for original ideas for her videos. When she found out about the TikTok Christmas challenge to create creative and festive Christmas-themed videos, she decided to take part.

Among the many participants was Julien, a TikToker known for his humorous and engaging videos. Élodie came across one of his challenge videos, in which he comically interpreted a Christmas song. She was immediately charmed by his sense of humor and creativity.

Élodie left a comment under Julien's video, complimenting its originality. To her surprise, Julien quickly replied, initiating a friendly and playful exchange of comments. Soon, they were following each other's content and interacting regularly.

Their Christmas videos, each with its own personal touch, increasingly captivated their respective subscribers. Their exchanges on TikTok became the highlight of their day, filled with humor and a budding complicity.

Encouraged by their subscribers, Élodie and Julien decided to collaborate on a Christmas video. Their first videoconference brainstorming session was a mix of creative ideas and laughter. They were amazed by the ease with which they worked together, and by the alchemy that developed between them.

Their collaborative video was an instant success, combining Julien's humor and Élodie's creativity. Their complicity was obvious, attracting attention and compliments from their communities.

Following the success of their collaboration, Élodie and Julien decided to meet in person to celebrate Christmas together. They chose a traditional Christmas market as their meeting point, the perfect place to capture the holiday spirit.

When they saw each other for the first time, there was an immediate moment of recognition, followed by an exchange of warm smiles. Their online complicity quickly turned into a real, tangible connection.

Wandering between the stalls of the Christmas market, Élodie and Julien shared hot chestnuts, laughed under the twinkling lights and filmed spontaneous moments for their TikToks. They discovered that they shared many interests beyond TikTok, including a love of music, art and travel.

Their day together was a perfect blend of work and pleasure, and the boundary between the two seemed to blur naturally. There was an undeniable chemistry between them, reinforced by the festive atmosphere.

As evening fell on the Christmas market, Élodie and Julien stopped to admire the large illuminated fir tree. In this enchanting setting, Julien took Élodie's hand.

"I never thought TikTok would lead me to meet someone as amazing as you," he says, his gaze locked in Elodie's.

Élodie smiled, her eyes shining with emotion. "Me neither, Julien. I'm so happy we met."

They vowed to continue creating not only videos, but memories together. Their participation in the TikTok Christmas challenge had been the beginning of a beautiful love story, an unexpected romance born of their shared passion for creativity and the holiday spirit.

Love Story

Mia, an artist and influencer on Instagram, loved sharing moments from her life through captivating stories. As Christmas approached, she began a series of daily stories, sharing moments of holiday preparation, decorating tips, and traditional recipes.

Among her many subscribers, Max, a professional photographer, was drawn to Mia's stories. He was charmed by her aesthetic sense, her authenticity and the way she captured the spirit of Christmas.

Max began interacting with Mia's stories, leaving comments and suggestions. Mia, intrigued by his thoughtful responses and artistic eye, visited his profile and was impressed by his photographs.

They began exchanging private messages, sharing their love of art, photography and the magic of Christmas. Their conversations were lively and mutually inspiring.

As the days went by, their virtual relationship grew stronger. Mia was touched by Max's sensitivity and creativity. She decided to invite him for a live collaboration for one of her Christmas stories.

Max enthusiastically accepted, delighted at the prospect of meeting Mia in person and sharing a creative moment together.

On the day of their collaboration, Mia and Max met in a charming café decorated for Christmas. From their first meeting, a natural connection and mutual ease was palpable. They discussed their ideas for the story, sharing laughs and creative insights.

The live story was a mix of decorating tutorials, Christmas recipe sharing and impromptu photo shoots. Their chemistry was obvious to all their subscribers, who reacted with enthusiasm and encouragement.

After the story, Mia and Max continued chatting, sharing a hot chocolate. They realized they had much more in common than their passion for Instagram and art.

"I'm really glad I met you, Max. You make this Christmas season even more special," Mia confessed, a shy smile on her lips.

Max looked at her, his heart beating faster. "Me too, Mia. I never thought sharing stories would lead us here."

As they parted, an implicit promise to meet again was exchanged. They both knew that something special had begun between them.

Over the following days, their exchanges continued, gradually turning into dates and shared moments. Their "Love Story" had begun as a series of posts on Instagram, but it had turned into a true love story, born under the twinkling lights and joy of Christmas.

Eco-Christmas

Anna and Thomas, both environmental activists, met during a project called "Eco-Noël". The initiative aimed to promote sustainable holiday practices, such as waste reduction, recycling and the use of eco-friendly decorations.

Anna, with her experience in environmental awareness-raising, and Thomas, a specialist in renewable energies, were asked to lead an awareness-raising campaign in their community.

Working together on the project, Anna and Thomas soon discovered that they shared common values and ideals. Their work sessions were marked by team spirit and a shared commitment to the environmental cause.

Beyond their passion for ecology, they found a natural complicity and ease of communication. Every discussion about the project strengthened their bond.

In the run-up to Christmas, Anna and Thomas organized several events for their campaign, including workshops on making recycled decorations and lectures on responsible holiday consumption.

These shared moments strengthened their bond. They

realized that they appreciated not only working together, but also each other's presence.

Anna and Thomas, both environmental activists, met during a project called "Eco-Noël". The initiative aimed to promote sustainable holiday practices, such as waste reduction, recycling and the use of eco-friendly decorations.

Anna, with her experience in environmental awareness-raising, and Thomas, a specialist in renewable energies, were asked to lead an awareness-raising campaign in their community.

Working together on the project, Anna and Thomas soon discovered that they shared common values and ideals. Their work sessions were marked by team spirit and a shared commitment to the environmental cause.

Beyond their passion for ecology, they found a natural complicity and ease of communication. Every discussion about the project strengthened their bond.

In the run-up to Christmas, Anna and Thomas organized several events for their campaign, including workshops on making recycled decorations and lectures on responsible holiday consumption.

These shared moments strengthened their bond. They realized that they appreciated not only working together, but also each other's presence.

Online Concert

Lucas, an independent musician, decided to organize a special Christmas online concert, offering his fans an intimate musical performance from his festively decorated living room. He announced the event on his social networks, attracting the attention of many fans, including Élise.

Élise, a great admirer of Lucas' music, was thrilled by the opportunity to see him play live, even virtually. She admired not only his talent, but also the passion and emotion he transmitted through his music.

On the evening of the concert, Élise logged on, looking forward to the musical experience. Lucas began his performance, captivating his audience with his melodies and warm voice. Between songs, he shared personal anecdotes and interacted with his fans' comments.

Élise was touched by Lucas's performance. She commented, "Your music lights up this Christmas evening. Thank you for this magical moment." Lucas read his comment aloud and thanked Élise, a sincere smile on his lips.

After the concert, Élise sent Lucas a message to thank him personally. To her surprise, he replied, and a conversation ensued between them. They discussed music, their Christmas experiences and their passions.

Their exchange continued over the days, moving from discussions about music to more personal sharing. There was an obvious chemistry between them, a bond that grew stronger with each exchange.

As the weeks went by, the exchanges between Lucas and Élise turned into regular conversations. They shared video calls, discussing anything and everything, often late into the night. Their connection seemed to defy distance, uniting two hearts across the screen.

Élise discovered that Lucas was more than just her favorite musician; he was a person with whom she shared values, laughter and dreams. For Lucas, Élise had become a source of inspiration and joy, far more than just a fan.

As Christmas approached, Lucas offered Elise a private concert via video call. "Consider it my Christmas present to you," he said.

On the evening of the concert, Élise got ready, excited and a little nervous. Lucas began to play, each song seeming to tell a part of their budding story. It was an intimate and moving experience, bringing their hearts even closer together.

After the private concert, Lucas and Élise knew they wanted to meet in person. They arranged to meet in Lucas' hometown, where they spent a day together exploring the streets decorated for Christmas.

Their meeting was as magical as their virtual conversations. Laughing together, sharing hot chocolate and walking hand in hand, they realized that their love was real.

As they parted, they promised to continue making music and living together. The online concert had been the beginning of a beautiful love story, a shared melody that would henceforth accompany their lives.

Christmas Escape Room

Clément, a fan of puzzles and escape games, booked a session in a Christmas-themed escape room for himself and his friends. The day before the event, his friends had to cancel, leaving him with two extra places.

Not wanting to waste tickets, Clément posted a message on an online group dedicated to escape room fans, offering the extra places. Alice, a fan of puzzle games and the Christmas spirit, saw the message and accepted the invitation.

On the day of the escape room, Clément and Alice met in front of the establishment. After a brief introduction, they entered the room, greeted by festive décor and puzzles based on Christmas traditions.

Working together to solve the puzzles, they discovered they made an effective team. Their complicity and sense of humor facilitated their progress through the game.

As they progressed through the escape room, Clément and Alice grew closer, sharing laughs and successes. They were impressed with each other, not only for their puzzle-solving skills, but also for their personalities.

Clément found Alice an intelligent and witty playmate.

Alice, for her part, appreciated Clément's insight and kindness. There was a chemistry between them that went beyond the escape room.

In the final minutes of the escape room, Clément and Alice's excitement was at its peak. They solved the final puzzle together, a task that required perfect cooperation. When the door opened, signifying their success, they burst into joy, celebrating their victory.

As they exited the escape room, they felt exhilarated not only by their triumph, but also by the connection they'd made. "It was incredible," said Alice, her eyes sparkling. "I've never laughed so much and thought so much at the same time."

"I agree," replied Clément. "It was an exceptional experience, especially with you as my partner."

They decided to extend the evening with a cup of coffee together. Sitting in a nearby café, decorated with tinsel and Christmas lights, they shared stories about their past experiences in escape rooms and their interests.

Their conversations revealed many similarities and shared

passions. They discovered that they both had a love of travel, literature and, of course, puzzle games.

As they parted, Clément and Alice exchanged telephone numbers, promising to meet again for further adventures. As they parted, a feeling of anticipation and mutual affection swept over them.

The evening in the Christmas escape room had been the beginning of a special connection. What had begun as a simple game had turned into the beginning of a promising relationship, based on mutual complicity and understanding.

 *Your Opinion Counts!*

Hey, you! Yes, you, who've just taken this magical journey through the 24 Christmas stories. I hope you've enjoyed every moment spent with us in these enchanted pages.

Your opinion means a lot to me. It not only helps me to grow as an author, but also to share this book with other lovers of romantic and magical tales like you. If you have a few minutes, I'd be super happy to read your review on [name of the platform or site where the book is sold or reviewed].

Every word from you is a star that lights up the path of creation and allows new content to see the light of day. Your impressions, your favorite moments, how you felt... I'm interested in everything!

And who knows? Maybe your ideas will inspire future stories! So don't hesitate to share your experience and let your friends and family know about "24 Advent Romance Stories ". Together, let's keep the magic of Christmas and the passion for good stories alive.

Thank you so much for your support, reading, and Merry Christmas!

Jade Lavoué

Glossary

DIY: Do It Yourself

Refers to activities aimed at creating, repairing or making objects oneself.

Streaming ;

Online streaming and playback of multimedia data, eliminating the need to download data

Swipe :

Interact with a touch screen by rapidly moving your finger over it

Vlog : Video blog

A blog that mainly broadcasts videos, often posted later on social networks.

VR - Virtual Reality -

A series of computer technologies designed to immerse one or more people in a virtual environment.

Printed in Dunstable, United Kingdom